A WISH IS A SEED

JESSICA YOUNG

illustrated by

MARIA CRISTINA PRITELLI

CREATIVE EDITIONS

A wish is a seed

carried on the wind.

It sails

across deep waters,

drifts

through dark canyons,

glides down busy streets

where no one stops to notice.

It travels far on tiny wings–

dancing along rooftops

and dodging raindrops.

Until–

it tumbles.

Then it lies,

still

and unseen.

Waiting . . .

When the time is right,

it sends down a silent root

and pushes up a hopeful shoot.

which breaks through hardened ground,

stretches toward the light,

reaches up

and out, into the unknown,

blooms.

A wish is a seed

carried on the wind.

Text copyright © 2020 by Jessica Young ⚘ Illustrations copyright © 2020 by Maria

Cristina Pritelli ⚘ Edited by Amy Novesky; designed by Rita Marshall

Published in 2020 by Creative Editions ⚘ P.O. Box 227, Mankato, MN 56002 USA

Creative Editions is an imprint of The Creative Company www.thecreativecompany.us

Library of Congress Cataloging-in-Publication Data

Names: Young, Jessica, author. / Pritelli, Maria Cristina, illustrator. ⚘ Title: A wish is

a seed / by Jessica Young; illustrated by Maria Cristina Pritelli. ⚘ Summary: When

a child makes a wish, where does it go? Like a tiny seed carried on the wind, a wish

journeys through adversity, takes root, and grows. ⚘ Identifiers: LCCN 2019029221 /

ISBN 978-1-56846-338-4 / Subjects: CYAC: Wishes–Fiction. / Seeds–Fiction.

Classification: LCC PZ7.Y8657 Wis 2020 / DDC [E]–dc23

First edition 9 8 7 6 5 4 3 2 1